HARRY'S
HOUSE OF
INVENTION

BLOOMSBURY EDUCATION
Bloomsbury Publishing Plc
50 Bedford Square, London, WC1B 3DP, UK

BLOOMSBURY, BLOOMSBURY EDUCATION and the Diana logo
are trademarks of Bloomsbury Publishing Plc

First published in Great Britain in 2004 by A&C Black, an imprint
of Bloomsbury Publishing Plc

This edition published in 2020 by Bloomsbury Publishing Plc

Packaged for Bloomsbury by Plum5 Limited

A catalogue record for this book is available from the British Library

ISBN: PB: 978-1-4729-6755-8;
ePDF: 978-1-4729-6754-1; ePub: 978-1-4729-6753-4

2 4 6 8 10 9 7 5 3 1

Printed and bound by CPI Group (UK) Ltd, Croydon, CR0 4YY

To find out more about our authors and books visit www.bloomsbury.com and sign up for our newsletters

HARRY'S
HOUSE OF
INVENTION

RACHEL ANDERSON
ILLUSTRATED BY CHRIS JEVONS

BLOOMSBURY EDUCATION

LONDON OXFORD NEW YORK NEW DELHI SYDNEY

For Nguyen Robertson

CONTENTS

CHAPTER ONE

THE BASE CAMP AT THE TOP OF THE STAIRS

In Harry Spoon's near-perfect world, there were two tip-top activities.

One: eating hot baked potatoes.

Two: playing with his Medi-Rescue-Mission-Men.

He did other things too.

He fed the cat. He slept peacefully
each night. Several times a day he
helped his brother, Aidan, look for his
lost shoes.

Every few minutes he rescued a
piece of Medi-Rescue-Mission-Men
equipment from baby Bella's mouth.

He also ran useful errands for his mother: fetching paper clips, a dowsing-rod, some umbrella spokes, a plastic windmill, a hubcap, or any other bits and pieces that she needed in her workshop.

Among Lillian Spoon's inventions was a solar-powered baby buggy, self-opening curtains, disappearing sticking-plaster, and a paw-operated tin-opener for hungry cats.

She was now finishing off a shoe-seeking robot for Aidan.

Harry's father, Patrick Spoon, invented vegetarian recipes. Harry helped him, too.

Harry's favourite topping on a baked potato was crispy-kelp-and-ginger dressing. His favourite place for setting up base camp for the Medi-Rescue-Mission-Men was on the landing at the top of the stairs.

One evening, Harry had just set up a tricky incident for his Medi-Rescue-Mission-Men when he heard the crunch of snapping plastic. Another paramedic's arm was crushed beneath Uncle Harold's big boots.

"Bit old for playing toy soldiers, aren't you, lad?" boomed Uncle Harold.

Harry clipped a replacement swivel arm into the paramedic's shoulder socket but kept his lips buttoned.

Uncle Harold wanted to be an inventor too, only his ideas, like the singing kettle and the electric toothbrush, had all been invented before. Harry wished Uncle Harold didn't share their home. But Lillian said, "Custard's thicker than water."

"Harry!" Patrick called. "Time to lend a hand."

Bother! Harry thought, because he hadn't finished rescuing his team and he didn't like to leave them in their risky situation.

Lillian came down from her workshop in the attic. She had to step round the rescuers.

"Harry!" she scolded. "I've told you a trillion times! This is not a sensible place for a base camp. Please move your toys off the landing."

"Yes, Mum."

"A grown-up could easily trip over a Mission Man and fall down the stairs."

The entire team of Medi-Rescue-Mission Men nodded in agreement. But it wasn't one of the grown-ups who had the accident. It was Harry.

CHAPTER TWO

EMERGENCY STATIONS

As Harry reached out to save the last of the Medi-Rescue-Mission-Men, the figure swung beyond Harry's grasp. They both lost their footing. The paramedic landed safely. But Harry hurtled backwards down the stairs.

His elbow hit the ground first. Then his shoulder. Then the rest. The pain was like fire.

"Poor Harry. Better soon," said Aidan.

"Glug gloog," said Bella.

"He's very pale," said Lillian.

"Storm in a teacup, if you ask me. The boy's a regular fusspot," said Uncle Harold as he hurried back upstairs with a sly smile.

Harry's arm was out of shape.  "Maybe we'd better not try to fix it ourselves this time," said Patrick.

Lillian agreed. They should let the hospital sort it out.

Accident and Emergency was buzzing.

A&E

Victims from every type of home disaster were being treated.

A granny had knitted herself inside a stocking.

A baby had swallowed a jar of jellybeans.

A lollipop lady had caught her thumb in her jacket zip.

All were receiving chocolate drops and TLC.

Harry was the only patient with broken bones so the nurse was very pleased to be able to look after him.

"You choose your own colour for the plaster," he told Harry. "And today's special offers are nite-glo green or blood-and-thunder red."

Harry didn't care about colours.
"I'll take the red," he said miserably.

So his arm was set in a heavy
red cast.

Harry could hardly move it. It felt
like a quite separate limb.

Back home, his life was no longer near-perfect. The two worst things were:

First: the pain.

Second: the not-being-able-to-do-anything-for-himself.

"I'm just useless," said Harry.

"You can say that again!" chuckled Uncle Harold as he helped himself to the biggest baked potato on the dish.

All next day, Harry lay in the garden with the clumsy cast resting on the cat.

"I hardly slept a wink last night," he moaned. "So there's no point going to school tomorrow. I won't be able to do anything.

I wish I was a Medi-Rescue-Mission-Man. Then I'd just click in a new arm."

But Harry didn't believe in magic. He knew wishes were just words.

CHAPTER THREE

POTIONS AND PEGS

After Harry had been helped into his
sleeping-suit by the cat, had his teeth
cleaned for him by Bella and been
launched up into his hammock by
Aidan, Patrick came along with a
glass jug.

"Beddy-byes drink," he said.
"Specially for you."

Patrick often mixed unusual
potions, such as a teething syrup for
Bella and an anti-flea tonic for the cat.

However, he had never invented anything as thick and red as this before. Harry wondered what was in it.

"Well, I added hops for sound sleep. Spinach for strength. A teaspoonful of moon-sugar. And several other significant things."

Then Lillian brought down her latest invention. She called it a triple-function limb attachment. "To reach, grab or twirl," she said. It was made from two clothes pegs, four wire coat-hangers, a rechargeable torch

battery, six rubber bands, and some
disappearing sticking plaster.

"Wow!" said Harry. His mother
had invented the buggy for Bella and
the shoe-searcher for
Aidan. But this was
the first gadget she'd
made specially
for him.

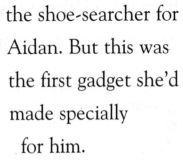

"Shall I
install it for
you?" Lillian
asked.

"And would
you like to try this
yummy potion?"
Patrick asked.

Harry had no time to wonder what
the attachment and the potion would
do to him before his eyes snapped shut.
He slept like a log.

When he woke, he felt ready for
anything till he saw his arm.

It reached to the end of
his hammock.

"Aha!" said Lillian.
"The triple-function limb is supposed
to have an exceptionally long reach,
an exceedingly strong grab and an
outstandingly speedy twirl."

At school everybody stared.
"Hey, Harry! Whatever's happened?"
they asked. But nobody listened to
anybody else because suddenly
they were all talking at once.

"My auntie broke her nose
playing tiddlywinks."

"My brother broke his arm
playing cribbage."

"My dad broke a rib playing dumb crambo."

Since everybody knew somebody who'd broken something, Harry stopped feeling unusual.

However, at playtime, he wasn't allowed outside with the others, in case he ran around and his arm bashed into someone.

He had to sit in the Quiet Room. Miranda was there too. She'd hidden her glasses again. None of the teachers could find them.

Miranda whispered to Harry, "They're behind the radiator."

At once, Harry's arm inside the red cast started to itch.

CHAPTER FOUR

INTRUDER IN THE NIGHT

The springs quivered. The sticking-plaster rippled, the battery glowed. The triple-function limb slithered forward like a snake across the Quiet Room as far as the radiator. Then it twisted behind the radiator. Then it made its exceedingly strong grab and suddenly, Miranda's glasses were safe in the grip of the clothes pegs. Then they were back on Miranda's nose.

Harry was highly praised for being so helpful.

But the triple-function limb had a will of its own. It dipped under the desks and with its clothes-peg pincers, knotted chattery Nathalie's plaits to the back of her chair.

During the afternoon, it moved on to the football field, grabbed the ball from the ref and kept it twirling like a planet just above the players' heads. They were furious.

On the way home, it darted into the open mouth of the pillar box, grabbed the letters, then twirled them high into the air like autumn leaves.

At home, it zoomed across the table, grabbed the biggest potato off the dish and twirled it so fast it turned to mash on the ceiling.

"Manners, manners," muttered Uncle Harold, who'd had his eye on that spud.

Lillian said firmly, "I know it's difficult, Harry, coping with a broken arm. But please set a good example to Aidan and Bella."

Harry tried to keep his arm secure in the sling. But the triple- function limb couldn't resist mischief. And it never ever lifted a finger to help any of the Spoons.

In the supermarket, it swept cheese strings off the shelves and juggled with Brussels sprouts. At the park, it threw Bella's dummy to the ducks, then dug for rabbits in the sandpit.

VEGETABLES

While Harry was sleeping, and couldn't keep an eye on it, the triple-function limb arm got into the most mischief.

At least, Harry supposed it must be the triple-function limb. Who else would creep about at dead of night to create such trouble?

Then, one night, the scrabbling was so loud that Harry woke.

To his surprise, he saw the triple-function limb lying on the duvet, quiet as a resting cockroach.

But the noise went on, like drawers being opened, shelves tipped over, and cupboards shaken. And it was coming from Lillian's workshop, as though something or somebody was on the rampage.

It was unsettling. Harry knew his mother was asleep. He could hear her snoring. Everybody was asleep, even Bella. Or nearly everybody.

Mission-Men, as Harry knew, should always be ready for whatever task came their way.

But what if it was a burglar? Armed with a big stick?

Harry thought he was too scared to move. But mischief and mayhem were the lifeblood of the triple-function limb. It reached out of the hammock, across the room, on to the landing, along the passage and up the stairs towards Lillian's workshop. Harry had to go with it.

And there, crouching behind Lillian's workbench, was Uncle Harold. The place was in chaos.

It was clear what Uncle Harold was up to. He was searching for something.

"How dare you!" Harry shouted.

Uncle Harold glanced round. Greed was in his eyes. Guilt was tattooed on his face.

"You sneaky thief!" Harry yelled. "You've been trying to steal my mum's best ideas, haven't you?"

Lillian's notebooks were flung about, her diagrams crumpled and scattered, her models set free and scuttling up the walls like crazy mice.

"It's not fair, not fair!" Uncle Harold stamped his feet.

Under the heavy soles of his hairy-wolf slippers another of Lillian's models was crushed to pieces. "Why does she have all the good ideas? I only wanted a few."

Before Harry had time to run down and fetch Patrick, the clothes-peg pincers had grabbed Uncle Harold by the scruff of his neck. And there was to be no mercy shown.

CHAPTER FIVE

UNCLE HAROLD'S COMEUPPANCE

Uncle Harold bellowed and struggled. But he was held too tightly to break free. Then the terrible twirling began. Uncle Harold was twirled and twirled like a human catherine wheel till his guilty eyes were popping.

"Put me down or I'll call for the police!" he bawled.

"Tip-top idea!" said Patrick.

"In fact, that's just what my clever wife is doing right now."

Lillian decided to try out the new laser-light alarm. It turned out to be most effective.

Two constables skidded up on their skateboards almost before she'd finished pushing the right buttons.

Uncle Harold was arrested. Tucked into his pyjama pockets and into his string vest were the plans for all Lillian's most interesting inventions.

"Oh, Harold, how could you?" Lillian said sadly as Harold was escorted away.

One of the best things about catching Uncle Harold red-handed in the act of theft was that Harry didn't feel useless any more. He was such a hero that a journalist came from the newspaper to take his photo.

Patrick said, "Sorry, but we haven't time to gossip now. We have to go to the fracture clinic for Harry's next appointment."

So the photographer took Lillian and Aidan and Bella's picture instead as "Family of the Hero".

Lillian was pleased. It gave her a chance to talk about the usefulness of her many inventions, though she decided not to mention the triple-function limb.

It now lay in disassembled parts in the waste-bin where much of it had come from in the first place.

Meanwhile, at the clinic, the plaster cast was sawn through. The top half was lifted off.

It was like opening the lid of a red casket. Harry held his breath. He was eager to see his own familiar arm.

He saw the cotton wool lining of the cast, so soft and clean. But what was that lying in the casket?

Harry and Patrick both gasped with horror. This didn't look like a healthy child's arm. It didn't look like anybody's arm. It was long, thin and pale, like a hairy maggot. Patrick wondered, was this the result of that unusual potion he'd mixed?

The nurse said, "Try to wiggle your fingers, Harry."

But Harry's fingers were as stiff as unused hinges. His wrist wouldn't move either, nor his hand or his elbow. Tears sprouted from his eyes.

His own arm was useless. He'd almost rather have back the triple-function limb.

It was wild but at least it was active.

But the nurse didn't seem worried. "This is quite usual," he said. "So you're going to have to exercise it, every day. To build up those muscles. What sport d'you like?"

"I used to play football," said Harry. "But I don't suppose they'll be wanting me back in the team, not after what happened."

"Another excellent exercise," said the nurse, "is swimming."

So on the way home, Patrick and Harry stopped by at the municipal pool. Patrick bought a group season ticket. And quite soon the entire Spoon family had learned to swim as elegantly as a school of porpoises.

READING ZONE!

WHAT DO YOU THINK?

Now you know what happens
in the story, start back at
the beginning of the book
and skim through just looking
at the pictures.

What extra humour do they add
to the story and the reader's
understanding of events?

Are there things you learn
from the pictures
that aren't
mentioned in
the text?

READING ZONE!

QUIZ TIME

Can you remember the answers
to these questions?

• What did Harry help his brother
find several times a day?

• Name three things that Mum
needed in her workshop.

• What did Harry's mum invent
for hungry cats?

• Why were the football players
so furious?

• What does the author say
the arm that came out of
the cast looked like?

READING ZONE!

STORYTELLING TOOLKIT

The author uses lots of
similes in the story.

Similes are when you compare
one thing with another using
the words 'like' or 'as'.

For example, at the end of the story
the author writes: 'the entire Spoon
family had learned to swim as
elegantly as a school of porpoises.'

There are lots of other similes
in this story to help the reader
understand things in more detail

Can you find some more?

READING ZONE!

GET CREATIVE

Why not create your own
invention to help with something
at home or school?

Think about something you don't
enjoy doing and what you could
invent to help with it.

Draw a design for your
invention or, if you have
time, you could try making
a model of your invention
using junk modeling.

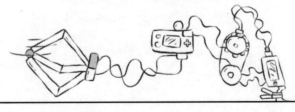